The AMAZING DAYS of ABBY HAYES

Reach for the Stars

Read all the books about me!

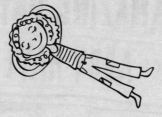

#1 Every Cloud Has a Silver Lining

#2 The Declaration of Independence

#3 Reach for the Stars

#4 Have Wheels, Will Travel

#5 Look Before You Leap

#6 The Pen Is Mightier Than the Sword

The AMAZING DAYS of ABBY HAYES

Reach for the Stars

ANNE MAZER

AN
APPLE
PAPERBACK

SCHOLASTIC INC.
New York Toronto London Auckland Sydney
Mexico City New Delhi Hong Kong

For Helen,

Purple pens forever!

ISBN 0-439-34122-1

12 11 10 9 8 7 6 5 4 3 2   2 3 4 5 6/0

Printed in the U.S.A.   40

First Scholastic Book Club printing, January 2002

Chapter 1

Thursday

"The play's the thing."
—William Shakespeare

Tropical Fruit Calendar

Hooray! It really _is_ the thing! Ms. Bunder and Ms. Kantor announced today that our class is going to put on a production of <u>Peter Pan</u> for the entire school. We will paint the sets, design the costumes, and, of course, act in the play! Everyone in Ms. Kantor's fifth grade will have something to do. I hope I will have a <u>lot</u> to do!

Abby Hayes, her best friend, Jessica, and their new friend, Natalie, sat in the school cafeteria. They pushed aside their trays and lunch boxes and cleared a space on the table.

"Okay, let's figure this out." Jessica pulled a pen from her overalls pocket, wiped an invisible speck of lint from the sleeve of her pale-blue sweater, and wrote "*Peter Pan*" at the top of a piece of paper.

Abby's best friend was always organized and neat. If you were looking for a ruler, an eraser, or a piece of paper, Jessica was the first person to ask.

"Yes, let's write down the roles," Abby said. She pushed an unruly lock of curly red hair from her face and peered at the blank piece of paper. "The tryouts are in two weeks. Let's figure out who wants to try out for which role."

Natalie nodded in agreement. "Then we can practice together." She was small and slim with short dark hair. Her blue sweatshirt had mysterious green stains on it. They were probably from the chemistry experiments she liked to do at home.

Jessica chewed on the end of her pen. Her asthma inhaler poked out of her overalls pocket. "There are a lot of great roles in *Peter Pan*," she said. "There's Wendy, Tinkerbell, Peter Pan . . ."

"That's who I want to be!" Abby interrupted.

"Can you fly?" Natalie teased her.

"I'll learn!" Abby said. "Ms. Bunder says you can learn anything if you try hard enough." Ms. Bunder was Abby's favorite teacher. She came to Ms. Kantor's class once a week to teach creative writing.

"I want to be John or Michael," Natalie said, "one of Wendy's little brothers. Do you think I could pass as a boy?"

Abby and Jessica studied her for a moment.

"If you combed your hair differently," Jessica said.

"If you put on boy's clothes," Abby said, "it'd be easy. I'd do it in a minute for the right role."

Natalie slicked her hair back. "There!" she said. She strutted back and forth in front of the table. "Now do I look like a boy?"

"Maybe *you* should be Peter Pan," Abby said. "Then you can fly just like Harry Potter does."

Natalie loved the Harry Potter books. She had read each one fourteen times and was working on her fifteenth round. "Maybe. But don't you want to try out for Peter Pan, Abby?"

Abby shrugged. "Either Peter Pan or Captain Hook." She waved her arms menacingly and scowled at her friends. "Captain Hook would be fun. Then again, maybe I should be Wendy."

Jessica pointed to the paper. "Let's get this all down." She began to write. "There's Smee, the Lost Boys, the Crocodile, Nana . . ."

"Jessica, you should be Tinkerbell," Abby said.

"No!" Jessica protested. "I want a quick walk-on part. You can be Peter Pan or Wendy, I'll be happy to be a pirate."

"Did I hear someone say 'Wendy'?" It was Brianna, the first girl in the fifth grade to wear matching nail polish and colored lip gloss. As usual, she was dressed as if she were about to walk down a runway. In spite of the chilly weather outside, she had on a cap-sleeved short black dress with chunky-heeled, bump-toed shoes. Her arms were bare, but that didn't seem to bother Brianna as long as she could wear the most fashionable clothes.

"We're deciding which roles to audition for," Abby told her.

Brianna smiled. "I've had the lead in every play I've been in since kindergarten. The role of Wendy is *mine*."

"If you're Wendy, I'm Tinkerbell." Her best friend, Bethany, giggled. Bethany wore a fleece jumper with a long-sleeved red shirt underneath. Her hair was long and blond instead of long and dark, like Brianna's. Other than that, it was hard to tell the two of them apart. "What a team we'll be."

"Ms. Bunder is going to decide," Abby reminded

them. "We all have to try out for the parts we want."

"I've auditioned all my life," Brianna announced with a flounce of her head. "I take ballet lessons and dance with the Hot Shots. I study voice, drama, and French. *Oui? Oui? N'est-ce pas?* Yes, yes, isn't that right?" she translated as her classmates stared at her in confusion.

Not only could Brianna speak French, sing, dance, and act, but she was the biggest bragger in the fifth grade. When it came to bragging, no one could keep up with her.

"Yay, Brianna," Bethany cheered.

"The role of Wendy was made for me," Brianna continued. "Or maybe I was made for the role of Wendy."

Abby exchanged glances with her friends. Brianna had been starring in plays since before she was born. If she wanted to be Wendy, Abby would be crazy to even try for the role. Still . . .

"Everyone will have a chance," Abby said, quoting Ms. Bunder.

"No one will have a chance next to me," Brianna retorted. "No one in fifth grade has the experience and knowledge that I do."

"Yay, Brianna," Bethany said again.

The two best friends linked arms and walked away.

"Weee, weeee, weee," Natalie said, imitating Brianna's French. "Isn't that what the fifth little piggy said all the way home?"

"We can't let Brianna annoy us," Abby said. She was speaking to herself as much as to Natalie and Jessica. "How much do experience and knowledge count, anyway? Maybe we're naturally talented."

"I don't think so," Jessica said. "I forgot my lines when I was a potato in my kindergarten play. It's all been downhill from there."

"I've never really been in a play," Natalie said. "This is so exciting."

"I've been in some skits," Abby said, "but this is my first time in a real play, too." Like Natalie, she found it very exciting. She hoped she could learn what she needed along the way. Not only did she want to do everything — act, paint, and help with costumes — but she wanted to do everything well.

This was a chance to show Ms. Bunder that she was good at more than just writing. Wouldn't Ms. Bunder be thrilled when she discovered all of Abby's talents!

"The idea of being onstage for more than a few

minutes makes me nervous," Jessica confessed. "I want to work mostly on the scenery and costumes."

"Not me!" Abby exclaimed. "I can't wait to be onstage!" She could already see herself. She would dance gracefully and sing like a bird. She would make the audience laugh and weep. Her SuperSibs would beg for her autograph.

"Is Brianna really that good?" Natalie asked. Her family had moved to town only a few months before, and she was still getting to know everyone. "Or does she just think she is?"

"She *is* a really good dancer," Abby admitted. "She's been in a lot of plays, too."

Jessica pulled her inhaler from her pocket and took a puff. "Don't worry, I bet you can learn your lines better than she can."

"We will!" Natalie and Abby said.

"Are you talking about the play?" Zach and Tyler came over and sat down next to the three friends.

"Yes!" the girls chorused.

"I'm going to be Captain Hook!" Zach announced. "With a computer-generated arm! I'm going to have it light up and make computer sounds."

Zach and Tyler were the resident fifth-grade computer fanatics — or gamies, as Abby called them. They spent most of their spare time in front of small square blinking screens.

"Smee," Tyler said. "Smee is me. Don't you think so?"

"Definitely," Abby agreed.

She wasn't going to tell Zach and Tyler that she was thinking of trying out for Captain Hook, too. They would just laugh at her. But why shouldn't she? If Peter Pan had always been played by girls or women, why not Captain Hook? All she had to do was pin up her wild red hair and hide it under a pirate's hat. She'd wear a black eye patch and a sailor's shirt. Tonight, as soon as she got home, she'd go up to her room and start practicing an evil laugh.

"The tryouts are in two weeks," Zach said, "and the play is in two months. That's not a lot of time. Especially if we're going to put it on for the whole school and our families."

This was another reason Abby wanted to shine in the play. Her family was good at *everything*. Her twin ninth-grade sisters, Eva and Isabel, were Super-Muscled and SuperBrained. Her younger brother, Alex, was in second grade and already a computer genius and a math whiz. Her father ran his own business, setting up his clients to do business on the Internet. Her mother was a successful lawyer. The Hayeses were not Type A's — they were Type A pluses!

Sometimes Abby wondered if she had been beamed in from another planet. She was *so* different from the rest of the amazing Hayes family. She wasn't a genius, a superstar, or even a highly successful person. She was an ordinary fifth-grader (with flaming red hair) who loved to write in her journal and collect calendars.

If she was a star in the play, she might prove, once and for all, that she really belonged in her family. Besides, neither of her older sisters had ever starred in a play. Abby would be the first Hayes to shine onstage.

The bell rang. Abby, Jessica, and Natalie gathered up their trays and lunch boxes and headed back to Ms. Kantor's room.

Chapter 2

My performance in <u>Peter Pan</u> will be a "thing of beauty." It will be a "joy forever," because my family will never stop talking about it. Neither will Ms. Bunder. The tryouts are in only two weeks. I must prepare myself in every way. Once I get my part, I will rehearse without cease!

But first I must decide which part I want. Captain Hook? Peter Pan? Wendy? Or any of the other roles?

Pluses and Minuses:

WENDY.

PLUS: A starring role. Get to be wise older sister and best friend of Peter Pan.

MINUS: Must compete with Brianna for the role. (She will be nasty if she doesn't get the part, and even worse if she does.)

TINKERBELL.

PLUS: Another starring role. No lines to memorize.

MINUS: Can't stand the name! Don't want to be a cute little fairy with wings!

MICHAEL OR JOHN.

PLUS: Get to sing, dance, and be on-stage.

MINUS: Don't want to spend the entire play in boys' pajamas.

PETER PAN.

PLUS: The best part in the play. Sings and dances and never has to grow up. Wears cute elf costume.

MINUS: What are the chances of my getting it?

CAPTAIN HOOK.

PLUS: Gets to wave mean-looking hook and menace everyone. Sword fight with Peter Pan.

MINUS: Will the boys laugh at me for trying out for this role?

When Abby came home from school on Friday, there was a letter waiting for her on the hall table. It was in a long, shiny envelope with pictures of cats all over the front and back. Her name and address were printed on a small white label. She recognized the thin black lettering right away.

"It's from Grandma Emma!" she called. Grandma Emma, her mother's mother, was her favorite relative. She lived halfway across the country with her dog, Zipper.

Abby wanted to tear the envelope open, but she didn't. Grandma Emma's envelopes were all handmade from catalog pages or old magazines. Abby saved them in a large manila folder. Grandma Emma had promised that the next time she came to visit, she would teach Abby to make her own envelopes.

She yanked open the drawer where her mother kept a letter opener, then carefully slit the envelope open. Grandma Emma's favorite stationery slid out.

Abby scanned the letter quickly and then yelled to Alex. "Grandma Emma is coming to visit!"

"Hooray!" he yelled back.

She ran to her room to check the dates on a calendar.

There were plenty of calendars to check. Abby had seventy-four. She had been collecting them since first grade. There was the Spuds Calendar she bought in fourth grade, the Polar Bear Calendar she slept with in first grade, and the Ancient Monuments Calendar her third-grade teacher had given her. Her newest calendars were the World Cup Soccer Calendar she had bought when she was trying out for the soccer team and the Genius Calendar Natalie had given her a month ago. Those were the ones she kept dates on.

She flipped through the pages of the Genius Calendar with its pictures of Einstein, Shakespeare, and Mozart. Maybe one day her sister Isabel would have her face on a Genius Calendar. Or her little brother, Alex. Eva was more likely to show up on a sports calendar. She was the captain of her lacrosse, basketball, and swim teams.

Abby marked the date of her grandmother's arrival in purple. There was another purple date circled the same week: the play! Wait until Grandma Emma heard! She would get to visit the Hayes family *and* see Abby perform.

Grandma Emma and Abby had a special relationship. When Abby was a baby, Grandma Emma had taken care of her every day. Plus, there was the red hair. When she was younger, Grandma Emma had wild, curly hair just like Abby's, though now it was white. She didn't collect calendars, but she had hundreds of salt and pepper shakers in her house. They were in the shapes of animals, people, and national monuments.

Abby unzipped her backpack and searched for the script. Now she was going to get to work! Grandma Emma would be in the audience the night of her performance. She began to read the play out loud, putting lots of expression into her voice.

Just as Peter Pan was about to confront Captain Hook, Abby's bedroom door flew open.

"Abby, have you seen my science notebook? I can't find it anywhere!"

It was her SuperSister Isabel, top student in her grade, winner of history awards, and school representative to a national debate in Washington, D.C., in a few months. Aside from being a straight-A student, Isabel loved clothes and fingernail polish. Today she wore a short suede skirt and a black Lycra top. Her nails were painted dark red to match her skirt.

"Haven't seen it," Abby said. She pointed to her writing notebook. "This is the only one I have. What about Eva?"

"Eva?" Isabel said. She stamped her foot. "Eva!"

"Did someone call me?" Abby's other SuperSister poked her head in the door. Unlike her more fashionable twin, she wore jeans and a T-shirt. Her hair was pulled away from her face with a sweatband. She was carrying a gym bag in one hand and a towel in the other.

"What did you do with my science notebook?" Isabel demanded.

"I haven't touched your science notebook! Why would I?"

"Because you were at the gym last night instead of studying for the test tomorrow! My notes are better than yours, and you know it!"

"For your information, I studied an hour last night from my own notes," Eva snapped. "Thank goodness I'm not an oversized brain in a glass jar!"

"At least I can think for myself!" Isabel retorted. "It's better than spending all my time trying to put a ridiculous ball through a little hoop!"

"Ridiculous? *You're* calling *basketball* ridiculous?"

The twins were like positive and negative charges. Put them together and you had an automatic explosion.

Abby held up the script. "I'm trying to do some schoolwork," she announced. "Could you go somewhere else?"

"I'm not leaving until I find my notebook!" Isabel exclaimed.

"I'm not leaving until Isabel apologizes!" Eva cried.

Abby sighed. Maybe she should go hide in the closet. Or lock herself in the bathroom. Or find a new family. One without twin SuperSisters who fought.

"Can someone make me hot chocolate?" It was Alex, their younger brother. He had a faint scar over his left eyebrow, where he had run into a slide. His hair was tousled and messy. His sweatshirt was on backward. At least his socks matched. That was better than usual.

"I will!" Abby jumped up, eager to be away from her older sisters. She picked up the script of *Peter Pan*. Maybe Alex would help her rehearse.

"Have you seen my science notebook, Alex?" Isabel asked.

Alex ran his fingers through his already messy hair. "It's in the kitchen," he said. "I was reading it."

"My science notebook?"

He nodded.

Abby held her breath and waited for the explosion. Isabel was very particular about her belongings.

"You were reading my honors science notes?" Isabel said again.

"Uh-huh."

Isabel beamed at her younger brother. "If you have any questions, just ask me. And next time, put it back in my room when you're done, okay?"

Abby stared at her older sister in amazement. Isabel wasn't mad at Alex for taking her notebook. Instead she seemed proud of him. If it had been Eva who had taken it, she would have blasted her with full nuclear power.

"You owe me two apologies now," Eva snapped.

"Do I?" Isabel retorted. "I don't think so."

Abby grabbed Alex's arm. "Come on, Alex! Time to make hot chocolate."

As they went down the stairs, Alex asked, "Why do they fight so much?"

"I don't know," Abby said. "It's just the way they are." It wasn't a good explanation, but it was the only one she had.

"In *Peter Pan*, the two brothers, John and Michael, don't fight at all," Abby told him. "Can you believe that?"

"No," Alex said.

"It's easier to believe in Tinkerbell and Peter Pan than in two siblings who never fight," Abby observed.

Alex grabbed her hand. "I'm glad *we* don't fight, Abby."

"Oh, sometimes we do," she said. "Just not as much as the twins."

It was hard to keep up with Eva and Isabel when it came to fighting. They probably broke a world record for it every day. She'd have to remember to put them in the *Hayes Book of World Records*. Eva and Isabel ought to win in the Frequent Fight category as well as Most Creative Insults and Most Fights with Fewest Reasons.

In the kitchen, their father was putting a roast into the oven. Abby's father worked at home in a converted attic office. Their mother worked in a big law firm and was often home late. She and their father divided up most of the household chores. Their father cooked, got the kids off to school in the morning, and shopped. Their mother did laundry and supervised the cleaning. Abby, Alex, Isabel, and Eva all helped out.

"Guess who's coming to visit?" her father asked.

Abby closed her eyes and waved her hands in the air. "I am getting an answer. . . ." she intoned. "With my psychic powers I will divine the truth. The answer is . . ."

"Grandma Emma!" Alex blurted.

Her father shook his head. "I thought I was going to surprise you two. I should have known better."

"She wrote me a letter," Abby explained. "I told Alex."

"Is she bringing Zipper?" Alex asked. He loved animals, but the Hayes family couldn't have any because of his allergies.

"No, she has to leave him in a kennel with his friends," their father said.

Alex looked disappointed.

"Guess what, Dad?" Abby said.

"I don't have your psychic powers," her father joked. "You better just tell me."

Abby waved her script at her father. "I'm going to be in a play, and it's the same week Grandma Emma is here!"

Her father pulled out the chopping board and knife and began to slice onions. "I'm sure she'll be thrilled."

"It's *Peter Pan*! I want to be Peter Pan or Captain Hook. Or maybe Wendy, if Brianna doesn't get the part."

"You'll be good at whatever you choose," her father said encouragingly.

"Dad! That's what you always say!"

"Be Peter Pan," Alex said. "He dances a lot. I saw the movie."

"Dad, can I take dance lessons?" Abby asked.

Her father smiled. "Why don't you get the part first, and then we'll talk about it."

Abby sighed. It was just like her parents to wait for results first. Didn't they know she had to start preparing *now*? She had to catch up with Brianna, who had been doing this all her life. Two weeks was all she had to get the perfect part.

Chapter 3

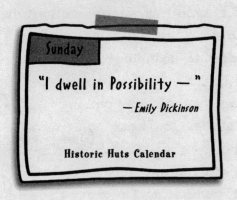

Sunday

"I dwell in Possibility — "
— Emily Dickinson

Historic Huts Calendar

I would prefer to dwell in Certainty.
Then I would know what role I am going
to get. Just to make sure I get one I
want, I am rehearsing several of them.
That is a lot of Possibility! It is also a
lot of work!

11 days until the audition!

Abby's Acting Practice Journal
Laughed evilly.
Hid left hand in sleeve and walked with
a rollicking gait.

Snarled.

Said "I won't grow up!" about a billion times.

Pretended to talk to fairies named Tinker-bell.

Practiced sword fighting.

Read stories to "Lost Boy" Alex.

Conclusion: I am very confused. Who am I? Am I mean and evil? A kid who doesn't want to grow up? Or a sweet older sister? (Ha! I wish I had one — or two — of those!)

News flash!

The Hayes family says it supports Abby Hayes's goals and aspirations. Paul Hayes tells his daughter she can do anything she wants. Olivia Hayes quotes her Working Woman's Wisdom Calendar about "reaching for the stars." Eva Hayes tells Abby to "go for the gold." Isabel says, "Anything worth doing is worth doing well." Alex

Hayes tells Abby that she will be the best ever.

However, when Abby Hayes starts to practice, the Hayes family becomes less understanding. They do not comprehend the demands of the stage. They do not encourage the young actress to reach perfection.

When Abby Hayes begins reading the script with a powerful, ringing interpretation of her three chosen roles, Isabel bangs on her bedroom door and demands that she tone down the noise. She says it's disturbing her study time.

Question: Is her study time more important than Abby's rehearsal time?

Another question: Is it possible to rehearse in a whisper? Whispering makes every line sound as if it's spoken by Tinkerbell.

Abby Hayes practiced dancing after dinner. Her own room was too cluttered with clothes on the floor, books, and piles of calendars to do more than a quick tiptoe across it, so she went into the living room.

She did pirouettes and pliés. She leaped across the room.

Instead of offering encouragement and praise, her SuperSister Eva told Abby to stop crashing into the furniture. She said it made her dizzy to watch. She said she was going to do calisthenics and the living room was reserved for _her_. When Abby protested this injustice, Eva said she had signed up for the space two days in advance.

Question: Since when does the Hayes family have a sign-up sheet for the living room?

Prevented from perfecting her ballet techniques, Abby decided to watch the movie _Peter Pan_. She had barely begun to watch for the second time when her mother, Olivia Hayes, told her to turn the television off.

"I'm studying the film!" Abby protested. "This is schoolwork!"

Olivia Hayes was not impressed. "You've watched too much television tonight, Abby."

"But, Mom," Abby eloquently argued.

Sign up now!
Couch _____
TV _____
Floor _____
Recliner_____

"There's a historical drama on in fifteen minutes," Isabel interrupted. "I'm not missing it! It's about the Hundred Years' War."

"Wait a minute!" Eva said. "_I'm_ planning to watch basketball."

"Too bad," Isabel said, turning the television to her channel.

Eva changed the channel again.

Question: Why isn't there a sign-up sheet for the television?

Abby did not stay to see what was going to happen. She did not want to be hit with a piece of shrapnel from the Hundred Years' War — or the Hundred Wars of Eva and Isabel. She left for her room.

After the play, the Hayes family will line up outside Abby's dressing room to apologize. She will graciously forgive them — after reminding them how they failed to recognize her acting genius.

P.S. Someone should issue frequent fighters coupons to my sisters. For every hundred fights, win a free fight or the argument of your choice.

Frequent Fighter Coupon
for every 100 fights
win a free fight
or the argument of your choice!

Sign up today!!!

• • •

In the afternoon, I went to Jessica's house to rehearse.

Good thing.

Jessica has no annoying older sisters.

We made all the noise we wanted, and her mother didn't complain. (It helped that she was in the basement doing laundry.)

Natalie came over in the middle of the

 afternoon. She said her parents are threatening to make her join the basketball team. They think she spends too much time in her room doing experiments and reading Harry Potter books.

Natalie put on green leggings and stood on the couch, pretending to be Peter Pan. We thought she was! She inspired me to new heights as Captain

Hook. Or maybe new depths.

Then we switched roles. I was Peter Pan and she was Captain Hook. That was fun, too. Jessica narrated the story with a wheeze. It was hard for her to breathe because of an asthma attack the night before.

After we rehearsed, we had cookies and hot chocolate. Jessica makes great hot chocolate!

I need to do a lot more work on my singing, dancing, and acting to be ready to meet the Brianna challenge at the audition. With the help of my friends, I will succeed.

After dinner tonight, made second request for dance lessons. No luck. Will get dance video from library instead.

Chapter 4

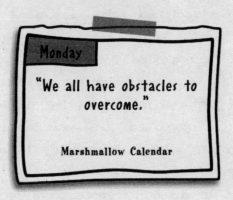

Monday

"We all have obstacles to overcome."

Marshmallow Calendar

Boy, do we ever! Why doesn't anyone ever tell us <u>how</u> to overcome the obstacles?? Huh? I want to know!! They just tell us that the obstacles are there. That's NOT a lot of help. Someone ought to have figured that out by now.

What I'd really like is a Solution-a-Day Calendar. Or an Answer to Every Problem Calendar. If they had a fifth-grade girls' edition, I'd buy a hundred copies!

Audition countdown: 10 days!

My problems:

To learn to sing, dance, and act in under two weeks!

To wow Ms. Bunder and Ms. Kantor with my reading.

To get a starring role in the play!

To dazzle everyone with my performance—especially Grandma Emma.

My solutions:

Took allowance and bought Ballet Calendar (identical to one I gave Brianna for her birthday), Sopranos of the South Calendar, and Peter Pan Calendar. Am studying them for clues that will help in my performance.

Watched dance video. Tried to imitate dancers' movements. Graceful arm gestures, toes pointed out, sudden leaps.

On third leap, banged leg on table. Got black-and-blue mark on shin.

Decided to sing instead. Put on tape of music for <u>Peter Pan</u>. Sang along.

Couldn't hit high notes. Squeaked and squawked.

Decided to practice breathing exercises that singers do, instead. Breathed deeply. Inhale, exhale. Inhale, exhale. Got dizzy. Fell on floor.

Decided to stop practicing.

Wrote letter to Grandma Emma instead.

Ms. Kantor, the fifth-grade-classroom teacher, clapped her hands. "All right! Everyone return to their desks!" she said.

The reading groups broke up. Abby gathered up her papers, returned a book to the shelf, and went back to her desk.

"Ms. Kantor! Ms. Kantor!" Brianna raised her hand.

"Yes, Brianna?" Ms. Kantor wore slacks and a sweater and comfortable sneakers. She had blond hair and a pointy nose. She had transferred from Swiss Hill Elementary; this was her first year at Lancaster.

Abby was glad that Ms. Kantor was new to their

school; it was good to have a teacher who didn't rave about her older sisters. To Ms. Kantor, Abby was just another student. She didn't have to live up to the megabrain of Isabel, or the megamuscles of Eva.

Brianna flipped her shiny dark hair over her shoulder. "Could we have an acting class? Not for me, of course." She smiled. "I've been taking classes since I was four. But some of the kids here don't have any idea how to read or rehearse. I want to make sure I act in a really professional production."

Ms. Kantor nodded her head. "That's a good idea, Brianna. We're going to work on geography projects next. Afterward, we'll have time to talk about the play. Maybe you can give everyone some acting tips."

"I'd love to, Ms. Kantor," Brianna smirked.

Abby pulled her journal onto her lap.

What are Brianna's acting tips? Always be the best? Make sure everyone knows it?

How can we all be the best when _she's_ the best? Maybe we have to be second best. Does that mean we try

harder? Or that Brianna brags harder?

I agree with Brianna. An acting class would be great. But I don't want Brianna teaching it.

As Ms. Kantor passed out sheets of paper for the geography project, Zach hummed the pirate song from *Peter Pan*.

A mischievous look passed over Natalie's face. She slipped her hand inside her desk. A tiny bell sounded.

"We have Tinkerbell with us today," Ms. Kantor observed. "I'm glad to see so much enthusiasm for the play. Hold on to it for another hour."

Zach stuck out his tongue at Natalie. She made a face back at him.

Brianna scowled at both of them. She didn't like it when Zach paid any kind of attention to another girl.

"Now, for geography this week, we're each going to create an island," Ms. Kantor continued. "I want you to map out fields, forests, hills, cities, and roads. You should use the symbols we've been studying. I want you to think about the climate of the island, too, as well as the kinds of food people eat and the clothing they wear."

Abby stared at the blank piece of paper in front of her. Normally, she loved blank pieces of paper. They were meant to be filled with writing. Writing was what she loved to do best. But this was mapmaking! It was very precise. She liked to draw, but she didn't like rules about what she had to draw. She wished she could write about the island instead of mapping it.

"We'll start today with sketches and a rough draft. Next Wednesday, I expect a full-color map with lots of details," Ms. Kantor said.

Next Wednesday? That was one day before the tryouts! As if Abby didn't have enough to think about!

"When it rains, it pours," she said to herself. She had read that this morning in her Cute 'n Cuddly Cat Calendar. Ms. Kantor ought to hand out umbrellas!

Jessica was already bent over her paper, sketching her island with a sharp pencil. She looked happy. She had already given her island a name, and she probably knew its exact population, chief exports, and seasonal climate. This was just the kind of assignment that Jessica thrived on.

Abby quietly opened her journal again.

*No wonder they call it a rough draft!
Maybe it should even be called a tough
draft! Or a rough, tough draft.*

*I don't want to think about this island!
I'd rather think about Mermaid Island, in
Never-Never-Land. Could I do a map of
Mermaid Island for the assignment? I
don't think so. Mermaids, pirates, fairies,
and flying boys are not scientific.*

Anyway, what would they export? Fairy dust?

"Abby?" It was Ms. Kantor.

She quickly shut her journal and picked up her pencil.

"Get to work," Ms. Kantor said. "Unless you want to do the assignment at home, where I won't be able to help you if you have a question."

Ms. Kantor didn't know about Isabel. Abby's older sister was a walking dictionary/encyclopedia/book of knowledge. Then again, Ms. Kantor was right. Abby had to work on it now. At home, rehearsing was her first priority.

"I can't think of what kind of island to draw," she said.

"You?" Ms. Kantor laughed. "With your imagination? Come on, Abby! You can do it!"

Abby stared at the blank piece of paper some more. Jessica had already started to sketch in rivers and lakes. Natalie was humming as she drew a mountain range, which she had named Hogwarts, after Harry Potter's school. Zach and Tyler were working on islands called Gamer's Island and Computer Paradise. Brianna was smiling as she drew Brianna's Isle. Abby couldn't see Bethany's paper, but she bet *her* island was called "Yay, Brianna!"

What should she do? She thought of her sisters. No, she didn't want to think of her sisters. They would do something perfectly wonderful, especially Isabel. Her father? He would map it all out on the computer. Her brother, Alex, would have every relationship of water, land, and people worked out, even though he was only in second grade. He would probably design solar-heated houses and gravity-powered wells, too.

When Ms. Kantor clapped her hands again, Abby was still staring glumly at her desk.

Jessica shot her a sympathetic look. "Don't worry, you'll get it," she whispered.

"Does anyone have questions about the map?" Ms. Kantor asked.

"Plenty," Abby said under her breath.

"Abby?" Ms. Kantor asked.

Abby shook her head. What was there to say? That her brain cells had gone on strike? That her imagination was out to lunch? That she had just experienced sudden brain failure?

She promised herself to work on the map tonight. Maybe one of her sisters, or even her little brother, would help her. There were times when geniuses in the family came in handy.

Five minutes later, Brianna stood at the front of the class, smiling smugly. "Observe," she said.

She clasped her hands, looked out the window, and began to speak.

"I wonder if Peter Pan will visit the nursery tonight," she said. "Michael? John? Are you ready to hear the stories?" She gazed lovingly at two invisible brothers, then took a deep breath, faced the class, and began to whirl back and forth.

"I can fly!" she cried. "I will never grow up!"

She mimed a sword fight. "Take that, Captain Hook!"

Brianna stopped suddenly, took another breath, then fluttered delicately around the room.

The fifth-graders watched Brianna in complete silence. When she bowed to the class after having done Wendy, Peter Pan, Tinkerbell, and Mrs. Darling in the space of five minutes, everyone began to applaud.

"Bravo!" yelled Bethany. "Yay, Brianna!"

"Well! That was *excellent*!" Ms. Kantor said. "Can you give us some hints about how to approach our roles?"

Abby exchanged glances with Jessica and Natalie. "Who ever heard of Wendy in bump-toed boots and rhinestone pants?" she whispered. "Or Peter Pan in a camisole?"

"I didn't even think about what she was wearing," Jessica said. "She's *really* good."

"Yeah," Natalie agreed.

Abby sighed. "I know. It's true. How will any of us ever get parts in the play?"

"She can only play one role," Jessica reminded her.

"It'll probably be the one I want!" Abby slipped her journal into her backpack. She couldn't give up. After all, anything might happen. Brianna might come down with the measles. Or twist her ankle. Or get laryngitis. In ten days, Abby might become an acting genius. Who knew what surprises lay in store for them all?

Chapter 5

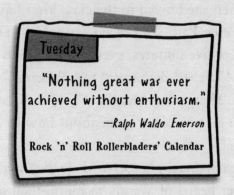

Tuesday

"Nothing great was ever achieved without enthusiasm."
—Ralph Waldo Emerson

Rock 'n' Roll Rollerbladers' Calendar

If that's true, then I should get whatever part I want! I have enough enthusiasm to fill all the oceans!

9 days to practice!

Pieces of acting advice Brianna gave the class: 3.
Number of times she said the words "I," "me," and "best" while giving advice: 27
Number of times she looked at Zach: 15
Number of times Zach looked back at her: 2

Roles she is going to try out for: Peter Pan and Wendy

How many others in the class admitted to wanting those roles: none

How many kids secretly want those roles: half the class — especially me!

Brianna's Best Acting Advice:
1. Observe others.
2. Use their mannerisms to bring characters to life.
3. <u>Become</u> the character. Think, eat, breathe, and laugh like the character. How would Peter Pan eat breakfast? What would Captain Hook say if he saw the SuperSisters fighting? How would Wendy do her homework?

(Note to self: Not good idea to do all characters at once. Might become split personality. Would end up in hospital ward. Would not be able to show up for audition.)

Maybe I should become Brianna! That is

the way to get her experience!
How to become Brianna:
1. Brag.
2. Brag.
3. Brag.
4. Flip hair.
5. Brag some more.

When Abby came down to breakfast, she was surprised to see her entire family sitting around the breakfast table.

"Mom?" Abby said. "Aren't you going to work?" Usually her mother had left or was leaving for the office just as Abby woke up.

Olivia Hayes checked her watch. She was wearing a pale-gray wool suit with a cream-colored silk blouse. Her hair was caught up in a sleek bun, and she wore a plain gold chain around her neck.

"Not this morning. I'm going to to talk to Eva and Isabel's class about what it's like to be a lawyer."

"Here you are, Abby," her father said. He poured her a glass of orange juice and pointed to a plate of French toast. "Help yourself. There's lots left."

"I invited her," Isabel announced. She wore a long

black velour spandex skirt with a jeans jacket worn over an electric-blue Lycra T-shirt. Her nails were painted blue to match.

"I made all the arrangements with the school," Eva added quickly. As usual, she looked as different from her twin as possible. She wore khaki pants and a zipped, hooded sweatshirt. "I made sure all the classes know about it. You'll have a big audience, Mom."

"Great." Olivia Hayes spread some jam on a piece of French toast. "The more the merrier."

"It was my idea in the first place," Isabel reminded her twin.

"Oh, yeah?" Eva retorted.

Abby's twin sisters were usually at the high school by the time Abby came down for breakfast. That was just fine with Abby. It made the start of the day much more peaceful and relaxed.

Their mother held up her hand. "Remember your promise," she said to the twins.

"What promise?" Alex asked sleepily. He was dressed neither for fashion nor comfort. In fact, he was barely dressed at all. His pajama top was half unbuttoned. He had on jeans, and one worn slipper on his left foot. Next to his plate was an old modem that he had begun to take apart.

"We're not going to fight today," Isabel and Eva chorused in unison. "That's what we promised as a thank-you to Mom for visiting the school."

"Wow," Alex said.

"It's a unilateral peace treaty," Isabel said as she poured herself a cup of coffee.

"It's plain old good sportsmanship," Eva insisted. "You shouldn't drink that stuff," she said to her twin. "It's not good for you."

Isabel glared at her. Instead of firing off one of her usual missiles, however, she grabbed the plate of French toast and helped herself to another piece.

Paul and Olivia Hayes smiled at each other. "Such a pleasant breakfast," Olivia said. "Thanks for making the French toast, honey."

Abby shook her head. She couldn't believe it. Could Isabel and Eva actually go five seconds without a fight? They needed to fight the way they needed to breathe. She had never before seen them exercise such self-control.

"Would you please pass the orange juice, Isabel?" Eva asked sweetly.

"Of course, Eva. Have another piece of French toast," her twin replied even more sweetly.

"Thank you, Isabel."

"You're welcome, Eva."

If Eva and Isabel could stop fighting for even ten minutes, *anything* was possible. Pigs could fly, the moon could be made of blue cheese, and Abby could be Wendy, Peter Pan, and Captain Hook all at once.

"Thanks, Eva and Isabel!" Abby said. "You're the greatest!"

"Sure," Eva said. She was so used to getting compliments, she never even questioned why she got them.

"Thanks for what?" Isabel demanded. She got as many compliments as Eva, but she always had to know why.

"You've given me hope for the future." Abby poured a generous helping of maple syrup over her French toast.

"Huh?" Isabel said.

Abby began to sing. "I won't grow up!"

"You won't grow up?" her mother teased. "Does that mean you don't want pierced ears anymore?"

"No!" Abby yelled. "I mean, yes! I *want* pierced ears. It's just a song from *Peter Pan*, Mom."

Her mother grinned at her, enjoying the joke.

Everyone was in a good mood this morning. It was probably because of the Twin Truce. Maybe now was the right time to ask for lessons. She had already asked two times. Maybe three would be a charm.

"Mom? Dad?" Abby said. "Do you think I could have singing lessons? Brianna's been taking them since she was three. She also takes dancing lessons, acting lessons, French lessons, *and* has pierced ears."

"A few holes in the head, huh?" Isabel commented. "Probably needs a place for the hot air to exit."

For once, Isabel had said something that Abby could agree with.

Her father frowned. "You can't catch up to Brianna in only a few short weeks."

"Lessons? For a school play?" her mother said.

"But I have to do something if I want to get a good part!" Abby cried.

Her parents exchanged glances.

"Please, Mom and Dad? Can I have *any* kind of lessons?"

"We'll have to discuss it," her mother said. "We can't give you an answer right now."

Abby's mother knew a thousand ways to delay committing herself to a decision. It was part of her legal training.

"Mom!" Abby cried.

"Wait a minute." Isabel blew on her nails and gave them a quick shine with her napkin. "I studied voice with an opera singer in sixth and seventh grades. Only five kids in my class were selected. Why don't I give Abby some singing lessons?"

Abby stared at her sister in horror. "Can't I take lessons with a professional?" she begged.

"Don't worry; I'm good," Isabel said confidently.

"I'm sure you are, honey," their mother agreed.

"We'll work on your breathing, your vowels, and a few scales," Isabel promised. "We'll start tonight."

Everyone beamed at Isabel. Especially Eva. "You're a sport, Sis," she said.

Isabel smiled between clenched teeth. Everyone knew she hated being called a sport.

"There's the solution to all your problems, Abby," her father said. "It takes time to find a good teacher, you know. Get started with your sister, and then, if you want to continue, we'll find someone to give you lessons."

The solution to all her problems? No! It was the beginning of all Abby's problems! Even if she was stuck on a desert island and her older sister was the only human around for thousands of miles, Abby *still* wouldn't want know-it-all SuperSib Genius Isabel to coach her in anything.

Chapter 6

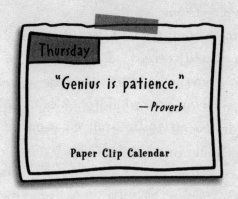

Thursday

"Genius is patience."
— Proverb

Paper Clip Calendar

Oh, yeah? Without <u>impatience</u>, nothing would ever get done. The auditions are only one week away, and I am impatient to master my roles. That is why I have done the following things.

7 days until A day!

Practiced <u>becoming</u> different characters. This is fun.

At breakfast yesterday, I became a piece of buttered toast. Felt dryness at my edges where no one buttered me. Enjoyed the feeling of melting butter over my middle. Cried when Eva ate me.

Was mourning the death of toast, when I became cold cereal. I was one of many marshmallow letters of the alphabet being poured into Alex's bowl. My friends and I tumbled together in the bowl, until suddenly I was floating in a sea of milk. Then a silver scoop pulled us out of the water and into the air, toward the wide-open mouth of a giant. Cried again when Alex ate me.

(My family now thinks I am crazy.)

Observed others. Tried to create new and exciting interpretation of roles.

Alex chews with mouth open. Will this be useful to any of my characters? Not unless I play Michael or John.

Eva flexes her muscles every five minutes. Very annoying habit. Who would do it?

Captain Hook? Play him as superjock who dislikes superbrain, Peter Pan?

Isabel constantly a) looks at her nails (to reassure herself they are still there and have not flown to someone else's hands?) b) blows on her nails (for good luck?) and c) buffs her nails (so she can use them as mirrors?).

Is Wendy also obsessed by fingernails? Does she check her nail polish as she reads stories to the Lost Boys?

Jessica fiddles with her asthma inhaler a lot. Does Peter Pan have asthma? Maybe that's why he doesn't want to grow up — he's afraid his asthma will get worse.

Asked Jessica what she thought of this. She said it wasn't realistic. Usually kids outgrow their asthma. If Peter Pan had asthma, he'd <u>want</u> to grow up!

Decided to use Natalie as model for Peter Pan. He is flying away from parents who make him join sports teams even though he hates sports. Must go to Never-Never-Land, where he can perform chemistry experiments and read Harry Potter books all day.

Watched video again. Noticed that Peter Pan brags a lot. Is it because he can fly? Or because he has a lot of Lost Boys obeying his slightest command? Reminds me of Brianna. (Except <u>her</u> Peter Pan would lead the Best Boys!)

Singing. This is where that "genius is patience" stuff comes in.

Especially when Isabel gives me a lesson.

She made me read the songs over and over.

"I <u>know</u> how to read," I told her. "I want to learn to sing."

"Speaking out loud is the first step to singing," she pronounced.

"I know how to speak," I said.

Isabel didn't seem to care.

After reading the songs out loud about a hundred times, she finally let me sing.

I started with the flying song. "Think about how it feels to fly when you sing it," Isabel said.

Began to flutter arms. Felt myself lift into air. My curly red hair fluttering in the wind. Just as I was really beginning to soar, I tripped on ball. (Why do balls lie around on floors, anyway? Sometimes it seems like they're waiting for you on purpose.)

Isabel said that I wasn't actually <u>supposed</u> to fly; I was just supposed to imagine it.

"Put the flying in your voice, not your feet," she said.

"What if my voice flies away?" I asked.

Older sister got annoyed. "I'm doing this as a favor to you, Abby, and you're not cooperating."

Must be very patient with Isabel when she gives me voice lessons.

(She thinks <u>she</u> is the one being patient with me!)

"I *love* her earrings," Abby said to Jessica as Ms. Bunder walked into the classroom. "Aren't they cute?"

"Me, too," Jessica agreed. She doodled a picture of an alien with long dangling earrings in the margin of her notebook.

It was Thursday morning, time for the weekly creative-writing class. Not only was Ms. Bunder Abby's all-time favorite teacher of her all-time favorite subject, she also wore great clothes and jewelry.

Today she wore a ribbed scoop-neck top and a long skirt with a daisy pattern on it. Around her neck was a silver daisy necklace. Her earrings matched the necklace.

Natalie nudged Abby and Jessica. "Look," she said, pointing to Brianna.

Brianna was taking notes on Ms. Bunder's outfit.

"I bet she has notebooks full of them," Abby whispered. "Maybe she opened up the June notebook by mistake this week; that's why she keeps wearing sleeveless dresses in the cold."

Ms. Bunder clapped her hands for attention.

"I have your last assignment here," she said, pointing to a stack of papers. "You all did a great job."

That was another thing Abby loved about Ms. Bunder: She was so enthusiastic! She made everyone feel excited about writing and what they could do with it. Especially Abby!

When she handed out writing journals, she had given Abby her favorite color, purple. Sometimes she teased Abby and called her "Purple Hayes" because she wrote with a purple pen in a purple notebook.

Brianna raised her hand. "Ms. Bunder, instead of doing a writing assignment, can we work on our roles for *Peter Pan* today?"

A mixed chorus of yeses and nos rose from the class.

"Yes!" cried Bethany, Natalie, Zach, and Tyler.

"No!" cried Jessica, Rachel, Jon, and Collin.

Abby didn't know what to say. On the one hand, she needed all the help she could get if she wanted to land a starring role next week.

On the other, she did *not* want to miss a minute of creative writing. It was an oasis in the middle of a desert of math homework, spelling tests, and geography assignments.

"Sorry, Brianna," Ms. Bunder picked up last week's assignments and began to return them to the students. "This hour is for writing."

Abby breathed a sigh of relief.

"We're going to write letters today," Ms. Bunder continued. "If you want to write a letter about the play, go ahead."

"Ugh! My mother makes me write thank-you letters all the time," Tyler groaned. "I don't want to write any more."

"Let's have fun," Ms. Bunder said. "Be playful. We can write to a character in a book, to a favorite author, to a friend, or to someone we admire. Our letters can be funny, imaginary, or true."

"How about a letter to ourselves?" Brianna asked.

"Why not?" Ms. Bunder said.

"A letter to a computer-game character?" Zach suggested.

Ms. Bunder nodded. "As long as it's a letter. Remember: The purpose of a letter is to communicate. Think about what you want to say and to whom you want to say it."

That was another thing Abby loved about Ms. Bunder. She was willing to consider any idea, no matter how different. She appreciated imagination.

The fifth-graders picked up their pens and began to write. Everyone in the class had something to communicate.

Dear Isabel,
Thanks for the singing lessons. They are very good. I might even like them if someone else was teaching them. . . .
Dear Isabel,
This is to inform you that your services as a singing teacher will no longer be required. . . .
Dear Isabel,
You're fired!

She crumpled the sheet and got out a new one.

"Abby? You haven't started?" Ms. Bunder handed her a paper with a rainbow star on the top. It was last week's assignment, a story that Abby had written in the form of a poem.

"False start, Ms. Bunder," Abby explained.

Ms. Bunder nodded her head as if she understood.

Abby picked up her pen again. Forget about Isabel! She'd write to her favorite grandmother! Her grandmother was the main reason she wanted to star in the play. She'd be so proud and happy to see Abby on stage!

Dear Grandma Emma,

Do hard work and perseverance lead to success? If so, I should be a star very soon. . . .

The words came more and more quickly. There was so much to tell her grandmother! She wondered if Grandma Emma would read the letter to her dog, Zipper.

Chapter 7

I wish I was. Then Isabel would have to row over to see me. Maybe she would get shipwrecked on another island on the way over. Then she would give singing lessons to the fish. (Ha-ha.)

My dad said that there is an Isle of Man. Why isn't there also an Isle of Animals? Or an Isle of Plants? What about an Isle of Kids?

Speaking of islands, I better get started

on mine. Was going to ask Isabel for help, but every time she sees me, she gives me singing advice.

5 more days . . . !

Help! I am being pursued by a crazed older sister who makes me sing scales at the breakfast table in front of the entire family. After school, she barges into my room and tells me to breathe from my stomach.

Have told her I don't want any more lessons. She said, "Fine," but she keeps giving advice.

Have also noticed her taking notes. Is Isabel writing research paper with me as subject? Am suspicious. Am also dizzy from all the breathing exercises.

Finally got island idea. Will create an island for Grandma Emma. That way, will finish the geography assignment _and_ give it to grandmother as a present when she arrives.

My dad, when I told him, said that I had killed two birds with one stone.

"I'd never kill one bird with a stone!" I protested.

He said it was just an expression. It means accomplishing two goals with one action.

"How about two for the price of one?" he said.

"I'm not buying anything," I pointed out.

"Well, I like your idea of doing your assignment and creating a present at the same time. It shows that you're thinking. You have a sharp mind, Abby."

"Thanks, Dad."

Nice compliment from Dad. May forgive him for forcing me to take singing lessons from Isabel.

Note to self: Why are minds sharpened or dulled? Why are they compared to knives and not forks? Can a mind be piercing? Or scoop like a spoon? My mind is wandering like a cursor on a computer screen. Must click back on main subject.

What is main subject?

Abby's Acting Journal

Ha! Ha! Ha!

Peals of insane laughter are heard off-stage as Captain Hook waves his sword and vows vengeance on Peter Pan, the boy who spends all his spare time in the library and aces every test.

The soothing voice of Wendy, older sister of Michael and John, is telling stories about Peter Pan. She is sitting in a big, comfortable chair and looking out the window at the stars. Every now and then, she stares at her fingernails and blows on them to dry the latest coat of polish.

"Do you think I can fly?" Peter Pan asks Wendy. He needs to have his confidence built up.

"If you believe it, you can fly," Wendy says. She climbs onto a table, opens her arms, and floats across the room. Her glittery nails sparkle in the moonlight.

Peter Pan stares at her in awe. He asks her to come home with him to Mermaid Island, which he created for a geography assignment. (He got the highest grade awarded

in his school. No one had ever before created an actual island!) He tells Wendy he
needs her to round up the Lost Boys, who
have gotten, well, lost.

Wait a minute. Wait a minute! <u>WAIT</u> a
minute!
I am not preparing my roles; I am
rewriting the play!!!
Must concentrate.
Must focus.
Must practice parts as they <u>are</u>; not as
they could be!
I can do it, I can, I can! If I believe
it, I can fly <u>and</u> act.

Decided to call friends and rehearse with
them to keep me on track.
Jessica was about to go shopping with
her mother for winter boots and couldn't
rehearse.
Natalie was free. She came over with
props: a sword, a pirate hat, and a cape.
(They were from her brother's room; he is at

boarding school, so he won't find out. Some people are lucky. They don't live with older siblings who make their lives miserable.)

Told Natalie about the changes I wanted to make to play. "I think Peter Pan is a brain who ran away from home," I said. "And Wendy is a know-it-all who checks her nail polish every fifteen minutes."

Natalie laughed. She thought it was funny but agreed we should rehearse the play as it was. Otherwise we might not get the parts we want.

Rehearsed play in my living room. (No SuperSibs in sight. They were at games, libraries, and friends' houses.)

Dad came in when we were rehearsing the sword-fight scene and watched for a while. He told me I am improving.

Hooray!

Then he asked Natalie what part she was trying out for.

"John or Michael," Natalie said. She pushed her short hair back from her face.

"Don't I look like a boy?"

Dad smiled and said, "You look like Peter Pan to me, Natalie."

"Really?" She thought about it for a moment, then shook her head. "I don't think so."

"You should try out for the role," my father advised her. "You're a natural actor."

Natalie looked at him like she couldn't believe it.

I couldn't believe it, either. My father was supposed to say those words to _me_!

"What's stopping you?" my father said to her. "Go for it! You have the talent!"

"What about me?" I demanded. "I want to be Peter Pan, too."

"I thought you wanted to be Wendy," my father said.

"That wimp?" I lied. "Never!"

"You'll find a role you like," he said to me. "You should sign up for an acting class," he told Natalie.

"What???" I felt breathless, as if someone had knocked the air from my lungs.

Was this how Jessica felt when she had an asthma attack? My father was telling Natalie to join an acting class, when he told _me_ I couldn't have one!

Natalie didn't notice that I was upset. She looked happy. "I act things out in my room," she told my father. "I pretend I'm different characters from the Harry Potter books."

"I'll be rooting for you, Natalie," my father said.

"_What about me_?" I said.

He gave me a hug. "Of course I'm rooting for you, Abby. That goes without saying."

"Brianna's going to be Peter Pan," I warned him. "She has years of acting experience. She'll get whatever she wants. Natalie doesn't have much of a chance."

"Don't be so sure about that," my father said. "Surprises happen."

Do they ever! Like fathers becoming traitors and encouraging friends instead of self!

Why My Father Encouraged Natalie and Not Me:
1. I'm so good I don't need any praise.
   (I don't believe this.)
2. She's not very good, and he was trying to boost her spirits.
   (I don't believe this, either.)
3. He's trying to break it to me gently: I'm a terrible actress and should give up all hope of appearing onstage.
   (This might be true, though I hope it isn't.)
4. He doesn't love me anymore and secretly wants another daughter who is gifted like the twins.
   (No comment.)
5. He thinks Natalie has lots of talent. And I don't.
   (Boo hoo.)
Pick the correct answer and win a trip to Never-Never-Land with all expenses paid!

* * *

It isn't Natalie's fault. She is really a nice person. She's not conceited at all —and still isn't, even after my father gave her so many compliments. I shouldn't be mad at her. I won't be mad at her. I won't!! I will be <u>really</u> mad at my father!

When will Jessica be back from her shopping trip? She has probably bought fifteen pairs of boots by now. I <u>need</u> to talk to her!!

No one answers at her house, so I have to talk to my journal instead.

Note to journal: Do not be offended that I sometimes want to talk to my best friend instead of you. Am sure you will be understanding.

Chapter 8

Is time my angel or my tormentor? Do I have enough time to make myself good enough to win a lead role?

Now that I've written to Grandma Emma and told her that I'm going to get a big role, I can't disappoint her. Or me.

Audition countdown: 3 days! That's all! I have decided to ignore my father. What does he know about acting, anyway? When I am a star, he'll be sorry!

Must become star of stage, if not screen. Must, must, must! Will, will, will!

"Practice makes perfect." That is what my mother always says. But <u>what</u> does it make perfect? My acting? Or something else, like fake crying?

<u>Abby's Acting Practice</u>

Hid in closet to avoid singing advice from Isabel. (She keeps telling me to sing numbers! What next? The alphabet?)

Fenced with Eva's lacrosse stick in front of mirror. Got it back in her room before she noticed that I had borrowed it.

Conducted secret acting exercises. At dinner, pretended that I had just arrived from Never-Never-Land. Laughed because of a joke Peter Pan had told me. Flicked fairy dust from my sleeves.

Family's reaction:

Eva: Do you have dandruff?

Mother: I don't know why you're laughing, Abby; you forgot to unload the dishwasher this afternoon. Now you'll have twice as much work to do after supper.

Alex: Will you play chess with me tonight?

Isabel: She can't. She has to practice her vowels.

Abby: I learned them in kindergarten.

Isabel ignored this vital piece of information.

Father: Is Natalie going to audition for the role of Peter Pan? Try to encourage her, Abby.

Excused myself from table. Went to room and read biography of famous actor who overcame discouragement and many obstacles to arrive at stardom.

"You're sure you don't want to come with us?" Jessica asked one more time.

"I'm staying in," Abby said firmly. She shuffled some papers on her desk. "I have to finish this."

"Okay," Jessica said. "I'm sorry." She reached in her pocket and pulled out a candy bar. "Here. Have a piece of this chocolate."

Abby broke off a piece of chocolate and put it in her mouth. She waved to Jessica, who put on her coat and scarf and went out of the classroom. Then she pulled out her colored pencils and paper.

It was recess, and instead of going out with her friends, Abby had decided to stay in and work on Grandma Emma's Island. She hadn't done a thing over the weekend, and it was due on Wednesday.

Ms. Kantor sat at her desk, eating a sandwich and reading a book. Abby wondered what book it was. What did teachers read in their spare time? Not stories about school, she bet. Ms. Kantor probably liked to read about people who scaled mountains or crossed seas.

The classroom was silent. Abby picked up a green pencil and drew the outlines of a large island that almost filled the page. Grandma Emma liked to canoe and row. She liked to hike, too. Abby drew a lake, a mountain range, and a city where her grandmother would live. The city had plenty of parks for Zipper to run in.

She drew a white sandy beach along the shore, where her grandmother would swim. She drew roads from the city to the mountain ranges and lakes and seashore.

Was this a warm, tropical island or a cold, arctic one? Did the people live by growing bananas and pineapples or by exporting wool? One thing was for sure: If you lived on an island, you ate lots of fish. Abby drew fish in the sea surrounding the island.

She was almost finished. Why had it taken her so long, and why had she thought the assignment was so hard? It had been fun to do. All she had needed was a good idea.

Reaching into her backpack, Abby pulled out a shiny envelope decorated with pictures of couches. It was Grandma Emma's latest letter. She had just gotten it that morning.

Dear Abby,

So you're going to be a star! I always knew it. Can't wait to see you in the play! Today Zipper and I went for a walk along the waterfront. Then we stopped in a café for blueberry muffins and hot chocolate. Did you know that your cousin Cleo is also starring in a play? She is the Tin Man in <u>The Wizard of Oz</u>. She wanted to borrow Zipper for the part of Toto, but I didn't think that Zipper would *behave himself onstage. He would probably bark at the Cowardly Lion or jump on the Scarecrow.*

Only six more weeks! I have the date circled in purple, just like you do.

Lots of love from your Grandma Emma.

Abby smiled as she read the letter again and imagined Zipper onstage. He was a small, excitable dog who barked shrilly when he saw a stranger. No one in her right mind would let him near a stage. She wondered why cousin Cleo had wanted him in her play. She wondered if cousin Cleo was a talented actress. Had her parents let her take singing and dancing lessons before she auditioned for her part?

Her cousin Cleo was also in fifth grade. She lived near Grandma Emma and got to see her all the time. Abby wished that *she* lived near Grandma Emma. Then she would visit her every day and play with Zipper, too. She might even get to take him on walks and feed him.

"All done, Abby?" Ms. Kantor put down her book, threw out the remains of her sandwich, and wrote the week's spelling words on the board.

"Yes, I finished!" Abby colored in the last flower

in the border of tropical flowers she had drawn around the island. Then she wrote "Grandma Emma's Island" in rainbow colors at the bottom.

Checking over the assignment one last time to see if she had forgotten anything, Abby carried it over to Ms. Kantor.

"Nice work," her teacher said.

"I'm going to frame it and give it to my grandmother as a present when she comes to visit," Abby told her. "Her very own island!"

"I'm sure she'll love it."

The bell rang. The fifth-graders trooped back into the classroom. Their cheeks were red from the cold. Laughing and jostling, they pulled off their mittens and coats.

Abby made a thumbs-up sign to Jessica. "It's done."

"Yes!" Jessica said. Behind her, Natalie clapped.

"Did I miss anything?" Abby asked them.

"Brianna gave us an acting workshop," Bethany answered. She was wearing a white coat with a faux fur collar. There were snowflakes in her hair.

Tyler and Zach were right behind her. Tyler tiptoed up to Zach, who pretended to menace him. "We're Hook and Smee, pirates to be!" they chanted.

Brianna made her entrance into the classroom. She had a long scarf flung around her shoulders like a boa. "You missed my master class," she said to Abby.

"I had work to do," Abby said.

"What part are you going to audition for — Mrs. Darling? Nana?" Brianna asked Abby. "I'll give you pointers."

"I'm going to audition for Wendy," Abby announced. "And I don't want any pointers."

"Good luck," Brianna cooed. "It's *my* part — unless I decide I'm Peter Pan."

Abby exchanged glances with Jessica and Natalie. Brianna couldn't have the whole play to herself — or could she?

"Our teachers will decide," Abby reminded everyone. She hoped Ms. Kantor and especially Ms. Bunder wouldn't be too impressed by Brianna. She hoped that she and Natalie both got good parts.

Mrs. Kantor cleared her throat. "Sit down, everyone. We have a new spelling unit to go over."

As the fifth-graders filed back to their seats, Jessica dropped a note on Abby's desk. She opened it up. "Meet me and Natalie after school," it said. "We'll

Chapter 7

Saturday

"No man is an island."
— *John Donne*

Continents Calendar

"Time is man's angel."
—*Friedrich von Schiller*

practice by ourselves."

Abby picked up her journal.

Brianna Brags Again! Wonder if she charged for her Master Class. Maybe she made Zach and Tyler give her cheat codes for computer games. Or did she collect everyone's ice-cream money?

Have decided not to try out for Captain Hook or Peter Pan. Will concentrate on Wendy. She is storyteller like me. Anyway, one role is more than enough to worry about. Especially if Brianna wants it!

Chapter 9

Wednesday

"Tomorrow,
tomorrow . . ."

—Annie

Days of Our Lives Calendar

My mother sings this song – and those are the only words she knows. When I tell her I'm sick of hearing it, she sings a song called "Yesterday." What if she put the two together – would she get a song called "Today"?

Today I am nervous about tomorrow. Tomorrow are the auditions. They are happening in the afternoon. We are skipping math and geography (hooray!).

Today is my last chance to practice before tomorrow.

1 day left!

Number of times Jessica, Natalie, and I have rehearsed the play together: 12 (a low estimate)

Number of times I have sung EACH of the songs: 31 (no thanks to Isabel)

Number of times I have watched the video: 11

Number of dance routines I have practiced every day: 4

Do all these numbers add up to a starring role? Or do they add up to disappointment?

When Abby woke up on Wednesday morning, snowflakes were coming down fast from a darkened sky. She rolled over in bed and picked up her journal. She leafed through its pages, reading once again everything she had written about preparing for the play. Then she got out of bed, pulled on her warmest sweater and heaviest jeans, and went downstairs.

In the kitchen, Isabel, still in her bathrobe, was pouring cereal into a bowl.

"Are you sick?" Abby asked. At this time of morning, Isabel was usually not only dressed, but in the library studying.

"Go back to bed," Isabel said. "A big storm is coming. School's canceled."

A snow day! Abby loved them. It was so cozy to stay home and watch the snow fall. She liked to drink hot chocolate and read a book and then, later on, go outside and help her father shovel snow. Today, however, she wasn't as thrilled as usual.

"Is it supposed to snow tomorrow, too?" She hoped not. What would happen to the audition if school was canceled? Ms. Bunder came only on Thursdays. They couldn't wait another week! If the auditions and the play had to be rescheduled, Grandma Emma might miss it!

"I don't know." Isabel took her bowl to the table. "You never can tell what these storms will do."

"It better stop snowing by tomorrow! Or else!" Abby pulled the oatmeal down from the shelf. The trees and bushes in the backyard were thickly coated with snow. Outside, there was no rush of morning traffic.

"Where's Alex?" she asked.

"Went back to bed." Isabel pulled out the world news section from the newspaper and began to scan it. She had painted her nails a pale shade of yellow the night before. "Eva's getting ready to cross-country ski with her friends. I'm going to study for the history debate."

Abby stirred the oatmeal in the pot and sleepily wondered what actors ate for breakfast. Did they have special diets like athletes? At least she didn't have to drink revolting power health shakes to become a star of the stage.

She glanced again at the snowy yard and hoped again that the storm would be over before tomorrow.

"I'll never trust the weather reports again," their father said, coming into the kitchen. "They said an inch of snow last night, and now we have a blizzard on our hands."

"Are you going skiing today, Dad?" Isabel asked.

"No, work as usual," her father said. "When you have a home office, you don't have any excuses. I have a new program that's giving me lots of problems. I'm going to try to get it up and running."

Abby sat down with her bowl of oatmeal.

"What about you, Abby?" he asked. "Going to spend the day with Jessica or Natalie?"

"Maybe." She hadn't completely forgiven her father. Natalie was a good actor, it was true; she just wanted him to be equally enthusiastic about her acting. "I need to work on my role."

"You've practiced and rehearsed very hard for two weeks," her father said to Abby. "You've done a great job. Today you should relax, forget about the play, and have fun."

"Do you mean that, Dad?" Abby cried.

"Of course I mean it! Take the day off, and tomorrow you'll have a terrific audition. You'll get whatever part you want."

Isabel dusted an invisible speck from her nails. "If I were you, I'd be using every moment to prepare."

"You're wrong, Isabel," their father said. "It's always good to take a break. Then you come back refreshed."

"Do you really think I've done a great job, Dad?" Abby asked again.

Her father nodded.

She jumped up and hugged him.

"I can't wait to see the play," he said. "There's a lot of talent in Ms. Kantor's class!"

Outside, the snow fell thickly. Abby finished her oatmeal. The day stretched before her, with nothing to do but enjoy herself. She would call Jessica and Natalie and invite them over. Maybe Natalie's mother would let her take a bus by herself, or maybe she'd drive her over. She hoped her friends would be in the mood for a good old-fashioned snowball fight.

Chapter 10

Rehearsing, practicing, and acting are <u>not</u> enough of a reward in themselves! I want more! I want to be Wendy. That will be my reward. I hope to have it by this afternoon.

Today is A day!

My father told me to "break a leg!" (Which one?)

Isabel reminded me to breathe. (Fat chance that I'll forget!)

Alex gave me his teddy
bear key chain for good luck.
My mother kissed me and
told me she knew I would do
well. (Mothers _always_ say that.
Why? And _how_ do they know?)
Eva was already at swim team practice,
so she couldn't add anything to the Hayes
family's good wishes.

I think I can, I think I can, I think I
can. Must remember I am Wendy, not the
Little Engine Who Could.

There is snow everywhere outside. We
have mountains of snow in the front yard.
But the sidewalks have narrow, shoveled
paths. The sky is clear and the roads are
plowed. School is NOT canceled. Hooray!
I can't wait to go to school today.

The Lancaster Elementary gym doubled as the
school auditorium. There was a stage at one end and
mats piled up at another. On Thursday afternoon, it

was filled with Ms. Kantor's fifth-graders, waiting to try out for the play.

Mr. Stevens, the gym teacher, stopped to watch the activity. "Can I have a part?" he asked jokingly.

"You can be Mr. Darling," Jessica said.

"He's the one who doesn't believe in Peter Pan," Mr. Stevens said. "I'd rather be a Lost Boy. They have all the fun."

"You're way too big," Abby pointed out. "You'd make the other Lost Boys look like dwarfs."

Mr. Stevens laughed. "I'll be part of the audience, then, and cheer the cast on."

Zach and Tyler pulled open the curtains.

There were stacks of chairs piled high at the back of the stage. Ms. Bunder and Ms. Kantor took two chairs and set them down near the front. Then Ms. Kantor clapped her hands for attention.

"Sit down, class!" she called. "Quiet, please!"

The fifth-graders sat cross-legged on the gym floor.

"Is everyone ready for the audition?" she asked. "Has everyone practiced their parts?"

"YES!" her fifth-graders roared in answer.

"Okay, let me tell you how this is going to work. We'll call you up one by one and ask you to read from your chosen part."

Abby, Jessica, and Natalie exchanged glances.

"While your classmates are onstage, give them your full attention," Ms. Kantor continued. "Clap after each person is done."

". . . and if you believe in fairies," Abby whispered to her friends.

"Tomorrow morning I'll announce the results."

A groan rose from the group.

"I know it's a long time to wait," Ms. Bunder said sympathetically. "Everyone will have a part."

Ms. Kantor added, "Not everyone is going to get the part they want, but we hope you'll be happy with the part you get."

"What if I don't get the part of Wendy?" Abby said in a panic to Jessica. "What if I have to be a Lost Boy or a pirate?"

"Don't worry," Jessica said. "You'll do great."

Abby closed her eyes, crossed her fingers, and whispered words of encouragement to herself. "You can do it," she murmured. "You can, you can, you can."

The audition began. One by one, the fifth-graders climbed onstage and read their lines.

Rachel and Jon read together for the parts of Mr.

and Mrs. Darling. Jon was a tall, husky boy with curly dark hair. He had a loud voice that boomed out over the gym.

As Mrs. Darling, Rachel, who was one of Brianna's friends, was brisk and matter-of-fact.

Ms. Bunder called Zach up.

He swaggered onstage and waved his left arm. A long hook protruded from his sleeve.

"I'm Captain Hook, and I'm going to get Peter Pan if it's the last thing I do," he snarled.

"Ooooh!" the audience gasped.

"He's pretty good, isn't he?" Natalie whispered to Abby and Jessica.

"Yeah," Abby agreed.

"I never knew Zach was so . . . dramatic," Brianna sighed. "Don't you agree, Bethany?"

Bethany nodded. "Tyler will be great as Smee, too," she said loudly. She glanced at him to see his reaction, but he wasn't listening.

"I can't wait to be onstage opposite Zach," Brianna said. "We'll have electrifying chemistry."

"The kind that explodes," Natalie muttered. "I know a thing or two about chemistry."

The reading was over. Zach walked off the stage, menacing the audience one last time with his hook.

The fifth-graders burst into loud applause.

"We'd like Brianna to come up next," Ms. Bunder said. "Are you ready, Brianna?"

"Of course I am," she announced. She marched onstage. Under her sweater and skirt she wore green leggings and a green top. In a moment, she had transformed herself.

"I thought you were trying out for the part of Wendy," Ms. Kantor said.

"I changed my mind." Brianna plopped a hat on her head, took a breath and, without a script, began to speak Peter Pan's lines.

"This is great for me," Abby whispered to Jessica, "but it's terrible for Natalie. She doesn't have a chance. Brianna is really, really good." She glanced at Natalie, who was watching Brianna intently. "I hope she's not too disappointed."

Brianna leaped across the stage like the ballet dancer that she was. She beamed at the audience. She sang in a high, pure voice, then beamed at everyone some more. Finally, she concluded her lines and bowed gracefully to Ms. Kantor and Ms. Bunder.

"Yay, Brianna!" Bethany yelled, clapping wildly.

With a gracious nod to her admirers, Brianna waltzed off the stage.

"I wouldn't like to play opposite Brianna," Jessica whispered. "She'd steal every scene."

"And say that it was someone else's fault," Abby concluded. If she got the part of Wendy, she might have to be onstage with Brianna. That would be the price of stardom.

"Abby!" Ms. Bunder was gesturing to her. "It's your turn!"

Her heart began to pound. Her head felt dizzy. This was the moment she had waited for. She rubbed Alex's teddy bear for good luck and got up.

"What part would you like to read?" Ms. Kantor asked as she climbed onto the stage.

"Wendy," Abby said. No one had auditioned for the part yet, thank goodness. If Abby had a chance to star in the play, this was it. She took three deep breaths, scanned the page that her teachers handed her, and began to read.

At first, her voice was wobbly, but then, suddenly, the words began to flow. She could almost see John and Michael opposite her, and even Peter Pan. She was aware of her classmates sitting on the floor a few feet away and Ms. Bunder and Ms. Kantor listening thoughtfully. As she read, she lopped off sentences and added new ones. It seemed completely natural to change the words from time to time. Wendy wouldn't say something this dumb, would she?

Then she was done. Ms. Kantor made a few notes on a piece of paper. Abby's arms and legs felt shaky. Above the applause, she heard Jessica and Natalie cheering.

"Very good, Abby." Ms. Bunder smiled at her.

She handed back the script, and weak with relief that it was finally over, she went back to her place.

"Great!" Jessica congratulated her.

"You were really good," Natalie agreed. "The best you've ever been."

"Really?" Her head was spinning. She was barely aware of Bethany, who was now onstage and flitting back and forth with a pair of pink fairy wings on her back. *"Really?"*

"Yes!" her friends said.

She sighed. Did other actors experience this when they got offstage? Were their legs wobbly, and did their heads feel like jelly?

One by one, the other fifth-graders paraded up onstage, read their lines, and marched off. Finally, Ms. Kantor called Natalie up.

"What part are you trying out for?"

"Peter Pan," Natalie said loudly.

Brianna smirked. "Poor thing."

Natalie was not in costume. She was wearing her jeans and a white sweatshirt with mysterious purple stains. For once, the stains were not from her chemistry experiments but from a laundry mistake her father had made.

Ms. Bunder handed Natalie the script. For a moment, Natalie stood perfectly still. Then slowly she began to move.

Abby stared at her in amazement. For a girl who hated sports, Natalie was incredibly graceful. Why had she never noticed it before?

After a moment, she forgot that she was watching her friend. She was seeing Peter Pan move and think and feel.

When Natalie finished, there was a moment of silence. Then everyone began to applaud. Except for Brianna, who sat frowning at Natalie.

"Is this the role you really want?" Ms. Bunder asked in a quiet voice.

Natalie shrugged. "Yes, I guess so."

Ms. Bunder and Ms. Kantor both wrote a few notes on their papers. Then they stood up. The auditions were over.

"Ms. Kantor and I are going to spend the next

hour discussing what we just saw. You've all done a great job, and we have some hard decisions in front of us," Ms. Bunder said. "We can't tell you anything now, so go home and get some rest. Ms. Kantor will announce the results tomorrow."

Chapter 11

Friday

"No news is good news."

Cube of Quotes Calendar

Is this true or not? If Ms. Kantor's class didn't have news, we'd go crazy. Now that we finally have it, we're still crazy.

The class is in an uproar — at least some of it. I don't know how I feel.

This morning we all got to school early. When the bell rang, the entire class hurried to Ms. Kantor's classroom. Ms. Kantor was sitting at her desk, grading papers.

"What roles did we get?" Zach asked. "Am I Captain Hook?"

"Take off your coat, Zach, and sit down quietly at your desk. Then we'll talk about the play."

"We've waited since yesterday to hear!" Bethany wailed.

Ms. Kantor nodded. "I know you're impatient. However, we have to wait until everyone is here."

We all had our coats and boots and scarves off in record time. (Will make <u>Hayes Book of World Records</u> as Fastest Fifth-Grade Dash to Desks.)

The last person straggled in. We rose for the pledge. Then we sat down. Ms. Kantor took the roll call. (We wanted another kind of role call.) Then she collected our homework.

(Note: Put in <u>Hayes Book of World Records</u> as Slowest, Most Agonizing Wait.)

When Ms. Kantor finally picked up her notebook and said it was time to tell us which roles we would play in <u>Peter Pan</u>, the whole class breathed a sigh of relief. Or was it a sigh of anxiety?

Brianna fluffed her hair.

Natalie was reading a Harry Potter book under her desk and didn't look up.

I crossed my fingers and rubbed Alex's good luck teddy bear key chain once more for luck.

Then Ms. Kantor made a speech about "how many talented students we have in this class, and how difficult a decision Ms. Bunder and I had."

"Translation," I whispered to Jessica and Natalie, "a lot of people didn't get the parts they wanted."

Natalie shrugged as if she didn't care. Jessica said, "Don't worry."

Finally, Ms. Kantor read the list.

Peter Pan Parts

(Note: Could this be tongue twister? "Playing a part in the Peter Pan production, Polly put a pint of potatoes in the pot."

Another note: Get back to main subject. Even if you don't want to.)

Most Exciting News: Natalie is Peter Pan!

Hooray! Hooray! She looked really happy.

Most Infuriating (but not Most Surprising) News: Brianna is Wendy.

Most Surprising (but not at all Infuriating) News: Jessica is the Crocodile.

Predictable News: Zach is Captain Hook; Tyler is Smee; Bethany is Tinkerbell.

Other News: Rachel and Jon are Mrs. and Mr. Darling. Meghan will be Nana, the nursemaid dog.

Most Shocking News: I will not be on-stage at all.

I am not Wendy, Tinkerbell, Peter Pan, Captain Hook, Smee, Mrs. Darling, Michael, John, or even a Lost Boy.

I am the Narrator. I will also do sound effects for Tinkerbell and the Crocodile, who don't speak, but ring and tick instead.

All my dreams are shattered. I am not going to be a star. Is it because I didn't have acting and singing lessons? I

don't think so. Natalie didn't have lessons, either.

Did Alex's good luck teddy bear chain fail? I don't think so. (But will give it back just in case.)

Was all my rehearsing and practicing for nothing? Don't want to think about it.

Now I have to face my family. They will all be eager to hear how I did. Don't want their a) sympathy, b) pity, or c) comforting words. Don't want to have Isabel tell me I should have breathed deeper, harder, and longer.

Grandma Emma won't see me onstage in a starring role!

Jessica says that the Narrator is very important. She said she's glad I'm doing the sound effects for the Crocodile.

Natalie sympathetic. Offered me half of her favorite dessert. Said that I had done a great audition, and she wished I had won the role of Wendy instead of Brianna.

Brianna not happy, either. "You didn't tell me you'd studied acting," she accused Natalie. "That's not fair!"

She didn't believe Natalie hadn't been taking acting classes.

A group of Brianna's friends went up to Ms. Kantor.

this is an injustice!

"Brianna should be Peter Pan," Bethany announced. "She's practically a professional! This is an injustice!"

"The role of Wendy is a major role," Ms. Kantor observed. "If Brianna doesn't like it, she can always be a pirate or a Lost Boy."

"Don't worry about me!" Brianna said quickly. "I accept the role of Wendy. The play must go on!"

Brianna got a starring role. My role is minor. The play could easily go on without me.

Chapter 12

Friday after school

"A hard beginning makes a good ending."

—*John Heywood*

Pocket Proverb Calendar

That's for sure! Especially today. See below for details.

At the end of the day, Ms. Kantor called me up to her desk.

"I know you're disappointed, Abby," she said. "You did a very good reading for the part of Wendy; however, Ms. Bunder and I have an important job for you."

Then Ms. Kantor told me what she and Ms. Bunder wanted me to do.

"The play is old-fashioned, and some of

it is outdated," Ms. Kantor said. "We
want you to rewrite it."

"Me?" I said.

"We noticed during the audition that
you made changes to Wendy's lines as you
were reading."

"Oops," I said.

"We liked the changes," she said. "We
wondered if you wanted to do more. Ms.
Bunder thinks that you'll do a great job. I
agree. What do you say?"

"Yes!" I cried, before the news had even
sunk in.

She told me that I could take the script
home this weekend.

"I know the play inside and out," I
told her. "I've rehearsed it, read it, sung
it, danced it, watched it, and dreamed
about it."

"Then you'll be able to get right to
work," Ms. Kantor said.

"Do I have to have it all done by next
week?"

Ms. Kantor reassured me. "Just get a

few ideas together. You'll be working on it with Ms. Bunder. You'll meet after school to discuss the changes."

Ms. Kantor gave me Ms. Bunder's phone number and told me to call her to discuss the play.

Yippee! Hooray! Zippety-do-dah! I WILL BE WORKING ON THE PLAY WITH MS. BUN-DER. Can things get any better?

Yes. I could have a part in the play, too.

This <u>almost</u> makes up for not having a starring role.

Chapter 13

So does Peter Pan.
That's all I can write today. Bye!!!

Busy, busy, busy, busy, busy, busy, busy.

Sunday (a week and a half?)

"Time speeds."

Dear Journal,
Please don't feel neglected. I still love you. But today I have to paint scenery and help with costumes.
Love, your best friend Abby

Wednesday

"Time gallops."

I am so busy writing, I don't have a chance to write!

Chapter 14

Monday | Grandma Emma
is Coming Today!

"Everything happens to everybody
sooner or later if there is
time enough."
— George Bernard Shaw
Baby Ballerina Calendar

What has happened over the last five weeks:

(Everything).

Number of rehearsals Ms. Kantor's class has had: 22 including 2 dress rehearsals

Rehearsals that took place during recess: 20

Number of kids who complained about missing recess: No one, because everyone wanted to be in the play.

Times Zach got carried away and menaced other kids with his hook: 5

Boasts and brags Natalie has made about having the lead role: 0

Boasts and brags Brianna has made about her costume and dancing, singing, and acting abilities: 1,000,000,000,000

Number of times Ms. Kantor said, "Thank you, Brianna, we are not on Broadway": 75

Number of kids and parents it took to make and paint the sets: 36 people over 2 days

What Ms. Bunder and I did to the script:

Made Peter Pan less boastful.

Changed a lot of the words so they sounded less old-fashioned.

Turned the Indians into space aliens, who try to kidnap Wendy and bring her onto their space shuttle.

Put in a lot more jokes.

What else I've done:
Painted sets.

Last Saturday, the whole class got together to paint an ocean with fish, a spaceship for the aliens, and tropical trees for Mermaid Island. Jessica and I painted Nana's doghouse bright blue. Then we helped Natalie make waves (ha-ha).

And I've also:
Sewn costumes (sort of).
Learned to play a xylophone for the voice of Tinkerbell.
Figured out how to use a metronome for crocodile ticktock.

Abby flung open the front door and threw down her backpack. "I'm home! Where's Grandma Emma?"

She ran down the hallway and into the kitchen. Her father and grandmother were sitting at the kitchen table in front of mugs of coffee and a plate of cookies.

"My baby!" Grandma Emma opened her arms and drew Abby into a big hug. She was short and slim, with curly white hair that had once been red and wild. She wore a blue suit jacket over a black turtleneck sweater and jeans.

"Grandma, I'm not a baby!" Abby said. "I'm in fifth grade. Some of the girls in my class already have pierced ears." She shot a meaningful look at her father. "If my parents weren't so old-fashioned, I would, too."

"It's just that we spent so much time together when you were a baby," Grandma Emma sighed. "I still miss seeing you all the time."

"Me, too!" Abby exclaimed. "I wish I was cousin Cleo and lived near you."

Grandma Emma gave her another hug. "I wish you did, too. I also wish you could get to know cousin Cleo. How long has it been since you've seen her?"

"Five years." Abby took a cookie from the plate and popped it in her mouth. She envied cousin Cleo, who got to spend so much time with her grandmother. She hoped Grandma Emma didn't love cousin Cleo more than she loved her. Wasn't there a saying that absence makes the heart grow fonder?

"You've grown," her grandmother said affectionately, looking her over. "That's a standard grandmotherly comment, isn't it?"

Paul Hayes smiled. "We would be disappointed if you didn't say it."

"You're becoming a lovely young woman," Grandma Emma commented.

Her father nodded his head. "I agree."

"Who, me?" Abby tried to remember what she had looked like in the mirror that morning. Nothing special, certainly. Just the usual nose, mouth, and eyes. Add in the unusual hair, and that about summed it up.

"Abby's been hard at work on the play," Paul Hayes said.

"It's tomorrow night, isn't it?" Grandma Emma sipped her coffee. "How exciting! I can't wait to see it!"

"I'm just the Narrator," Abby apologized. "It isn't much of a part. One of my best friends is Peter Pan."

"The little roles are as important as the big ones," her grandmother said. "No one can be on a stage all by themselves."

"You've never met Brianna!" Abby exclaimed. Still, her grandmother's words gave her a warm feeling inside.

"It's not what you are, it's who you are," Grandma Emma concluded. She rummaged in her bag and handed Abby a wrapped package. It was flat and square and light.

Abby opened it carefully. She had already guessed what it was. "Salt and Pepper Shakers of North America Calendar," she said. "Just what I've always wanted!"

Her grandmother nodded. "I wanted to remind you of me."

"I always think of you whenever I put salt and pepper on my food," Abby said.

"Because I'm so peppery?" Grandma Emma joked.

Her father laughed. "Is this like the fairy tale where the daughter tells her father she loves him as much as salt?"

"No, it's because of Grandma Emma's salt and pepper shaker collection!" Abby jiggled the salt shaker in the middle of the table. It was shaped like a mouse. The pepper shaker was shaped like a cat. They had been a present from Grandma Emma. "Now I'll think of Grandma Emma whenever I look at the calendar."

Abby gave her grandmother a kiss. "I have a present for you, too." She pulled Grandma Emma's Island from her backpack. She had had it matted and framed. Now it looked almost like a real piece of art.

"An island! For me!" her grandmother exclaimed.

"No one's ever given me an island before! Thank you, Abby!"

The front door slammed. Quarreling voices were heard in the hallway.

"Sounds like the twins," Abby's father said. "I knew the peace wouldn't last long."

"Hello, Isabel! Hello, Eva!" Grandma Emma called.

Abby's two older sisters burst through the door. As usual they were glowering at each other. The Twin Truce had been forgotten.

"Now, what are you two arguing about today?" Grandma Emma asked.

"Which would you rather do first?" Eva said. "Go to my games or watch Isabel debate?"

Grandma Emma gave them each a hug and a kiss. "First on my list is to rest from my trip," she announced. "Then I'm going to see Abby in her play. After that, I'm up for grabs. I plan to spend time with each of you."

Paul Hayes stood up and grabbed his car keys from a hook on the wall. "I have to pick up Alex from his swim lesson," he said. "We'll be back in twenty minutes."

Isabel took a cookie from the plate. "Did you make these?" she asked Grandma Emma.

"No, they're direct from the bakery. What's the latest in fingernail polish?" she asked.

As Isabel spread out her fingers for Grandma Emma to admire, Eva sniffed in disapproval.

"How about you, Eva? Any new sports? Let's see — you swim, run, and play basketball, lacrosse, and softball. What else?"

"Skiing and ice-skating," Eva said. "Do you want to come with me?"

"I love to ice-skate," Grandma Emma said. "Do they rent skates at the rink?"

Abby leafed through the pages of her new calendar. It was good to have her grandmother here. Everyone was happy. Even the twins had simmered down to an occasional annoyed murmur.

Chapter 15

Tuesday

"Reach for the stars."

Working Woman's Wisdom Calender
(As quoted by Olivia Hayes)

Yes, my mother said it <u>again</u> this morning! Well, I reached for them and wasn't tall enough to touch them. So I have to settle for watching the stars.

The stars are Zach, Tyler, Brianna, and Natalie. They will do a good job of acting tonight. All hope is not dead for me. I am only ten years old. Maybe someday, when I'm older, I will be the star of a tragedy. (Have had good practice with <u>Peter Pan</u>.)

Grandma Emma taught me to make envelopes last night. I made a stack of them

from Alex's nature magazines. I
now have monkey, lynx, cheetah,
antelope, spotted lizard,
grasshopper, dung beetle, spider,
eagle, copperhead snake, and
blue heron envelopes. Gave a
few to Alex so he wouldn't be
mad I tore up his old magazines. (He
doesn't read them anymore but says he
does.)

The doorbell is ringing. It's Jessica, come
to pick me up for school. She wants to say
hi to Grandma Emma. Have to go! Wish me
luck!

Half an hour before the performance was due to
start, Abby stood on the stage and surveyed the gym.
It had been transformed. All the chairs had been
taken off the stage and were lined up in rows. Now
they stood waiting for the people who were going to
fill them. It made Abby dizzy to think of all the people who would be here tonight — not just her family
and her friends' families, but neighbors, teachers,
kids, families from other grades, and the school

principal. There might be hundreds of people watching!

Backstage, Ms. Kantor bustled around, fixing costumes, soothing tempers, reassuring nervous actors, and telling others to settle down.

The aliens struggled into their shiny costumes. When they walked, silver bug antennae wiggled on their heads. The pirates adjusted colorful bandannas, while Zach, who wore all black, tugged on a pair of boots he had borrowed from an older brother.

"Look at Tinkerbell," Jessica whispered to Abby.

Bethany wore a pink-and-white tutu, with pink tights and ballet slippers. She had a glittery crown on her head and a silver wand in her hand.

She rose on her toes and twirled around the stage. "Don't forget to announce my entrance," she said to Abby.

"I won't!" Abby held up the xylophone stick. "It'll be loud and clear."

"Where's Wendy?" Ms. Bunder had an armful of scripts. "Has anyone seen her yet?"

"I'm here!" Brianna stepped out from behind the curtain. As Wendy, she was wearing a long pale-blue silk nightgown with panels of lace at the cuffs and neckline and matching ballet slippers. Her long dark hair streamed down around her shoulders.

"Does she wear that thing to bed?" Abby whispered to Jessica. "I thought she'd be wearing flannel jammies and bunny slippers. Or boxers and a T-shirt."

"My entire family is here tonight," Brianna announced. "Parents, younger sister, all my grandparents, two great-grandparents, twelve cousins, and four sets of aunts and uncles. Plus my neighbors and my mother's office friends. They've all come to see me perform."

"She could fill the gym all by herself," Abby murmured.

"Brianna, I have some small script changes to go over with you," Ms. Bunder said.

"Of course. I'm a professional," Brianna said.

Natalie adjusted a feather in her hat. It had been hard finding a green hat for her, but Abby had finally unearthed one in her sister Isabel's closet.

"Are you ready, Peter Pan?" Ms. Kantor asked. She was carrying a large felt crocodile head.

Natalie nodded.

"Are you nervous?"

"A little," Natalie admitted, "but I've got my lucky socks on."

"Lucky socks! I want a pair!" Ms. Kantor motioned to Jessica. "Can you put this crocodile head on by yourself or do you need help?"

"I need help," Jessica said.

Tyler peeked between the curtains. "People are starting to come in."

"You're on first, Abby," Ms. Kantor said. She fitted the crocodile mask over Jessica's head. "Do you want to review your lines one last time?"

Abby took a deep breath. She had written most of her own lines and then memorized them, but for a moment her mind went blank. She glanced at the script, then touched the new silver snowflake necklace that Grandma Emma had given her.

Ten minutes later, the lights flickered, then darkened. The hum of voices quieted. Abby stepped onstage in front of a packed gym.

When she sat down again, only a few minutes later, she hadn't forgotten her lines, tripped, stumbled, said the wrong word, or stared dumbly at the audience. Other than that, she wasn't sure how she had done. Everyone had applauded enthusiastically, but that didn't mean anything. After all, she was the first one onstage. The audience was probably glad the play had started.

"You were great," Jessica whispered from inside her crocodile costume.

"Do you mean it?" Her heart was still pounding wildly.

"A crocodile wouldn't lie!"

Abby picked up the xylophone and metronome and went to her seat in front of the stage to wait for Tinkerbell's entrance.

In the moments when Tinkerbell or the Crocodile were not onstage, Abby watched the play. No one forgot lines, and the fifth-graders acted their parts with energy and enthusiasm. The audience was enjoying it, too. When the aliens came onstage with their spacecraft lit up by a strobe light, everyone burst into applause.

Every now and then, Abby glanced into the audience. Her grandmother was watching with a huge smile on her face. Neither Isabel nor Eva seemed bored. Alex, her seven-year-old brother, was manning the camcorder, with her father right behind him. Alex knew how to operate the thing, but who knew what a seven-year-old behind a camcorder might do. He might zoom in on everyone's feet or decide to film the play sideways.

Finally, Captain Hook fell into the water where the Crocodile awaited him. The three Darling children returned to their home, where they were reunited with their parents and Nana.

The curtain fell. The audience went wild. They yelled, cheered, whistled, and stamped their feet, as one by one the players came out onstage for the curtain call.

Finally, the entire cast stood onstage in a semicircle. Ms. Kantor and Ms. Bunder joined them, to more applause.

When the cheering died down, the teachers came forward.

Ms. Kantor cleared her throat. "We'd like to acknowledge someone who made a very special contribution to the play," she said.

Who was that, Abby wondered. Brianna? Natalie? She hoped it wasn't Brianna. The acknowledgment would take a minute, but the bragging would go on for months.

"A fifth-grade student rewrote the entire script of *Peter Pan*. We think she did a great job. We'd like her to come forward now."

"Me?" Abby said. "You're talking about me?"

"Yes, you!" Jessica gave her a friendly shove.

She stumbled toward the front of the stage, where her teachers put their arms around her.

"This is Abby Hayes," Ms. Bunder introduced her. "Let's give her a round of applause. She wrote the very entertaining and lively version of *Peter Pan* that was performed tonight."

The audience rose to its feet. Cheering loudest of all were her parents, grandmother, and siblings. They looked proud and thrilled. Abby waved to them and beamed. Maybe she was a star, after all.

Chapter 16

Tuesday (night, after the play)

I don't need any inspiring quotes tonight. I am floating on cloud nine! Or maybe it's cloud ninety!

cloud #9

Standing ovations
Brianna got: 3
   Standing ovations
Natalie got: 4 (Ha-ha ha-ha!)
   Total strangers who stopped to give me compliments on the script: 32
   Cookies Tyler and Zach gobbled at the cast party afterward: 25 each (I counted)

Flavors of punch Bethany spilled on her pink tutu: grape and tutti-frutti

Number of times Eva asked me to do her creative-writing homework for her: about 6

NEWS FLASH!

There were many surprised parents in the

 audience tonight. Among them were the Hayes parents, Paul and Olivia. They regarded their daughter with awe and respect and said (with a touch of reproach), "Why didn't you tell us you were rewriting the script?"

Abby Hayes told them she wanted to surprise them. She also didn't want to disappoint them.

They were not disappointed. They said to Abby that it was one of the best school productions they had ever seen.

Natalie's parents were also shocked and stunned at their daughter's talent. They announced, in public, that they would enroll Natalie in acting classes immediately.

"Instead of basketball?" Natalie asked quickly.

"You have to do a sport, too," they said.

Natalie was not happy about that but may try to convince them to let her take a dance class instead.

The only adult not surprised by this amazing display of youthful talent was Grandma Emma. She said she knew it all along.

After the cast party, we had a Hayes family party. Hot apple cider, donuts, and tea were enjoyed by all. Isabel and Eva only fought once. Grandma Emma did a jig in the middle of the living room floor. Abby Hayes sang a song from <u>Peter Pan</u>. Alex reviewed the video-cassette of the play with the rest of the family. He did a good job of filming it!

Am very, very, very tired, and my head

feels like a beehive with lots of buzzing inside. Alex just came up to give me his teddy bear key chain.

"The good luck worked for you," he said. "You can keep it."

Gave younger brother a hug. Told him I will use it to try to get parents to agree to pierced ears.